THE

PEN-

VERSE

To _______________________

(Enter Your Name)

CHAPTER 1

INTRODUCTION

Greetings, character 102927b. This book is written in Greek, but it will hopefully be translated for you so that you can understand the content it offers. My name is D9NO K9NG, and I am a P5N GO4, a powerful entity with the sole purpose of helping my creator build his reality.

I am from a reality known as the 'Pen-Verse', where we use pens for creation and protection. I am well-known in my reality for my creative pen inventions, ranging from pens that are the size of three universes to pens that are powerful enough to destroy a universe just by colliding with it, and so on.

You might be thinking, why am I creating these weapons that could be used for destruction, and what's the purpose of numbers in my name? I assure you, there is nothing to worry about. I'm not sure if I can trust you just yet, so I have included numbers in many names. I am not evil, and these pens are not made for destruction, but for the protection of not just my Reality, but other realities too.

This book has travelled through multiple realities before reaching you, and thanks to my creator, I can freely communicate with you through the book. You may be wondering who my creator is. He not only created me but also my whole reality. He is one of the strongest beings in this story.

The truth is that we are all in a story, being read by someone above us all. We are not real creatures, just imaginary characters. If we are forgotten, we will soon disappear. No one knows about the fate of the forgotten, but to reduce the risk, we must create suspense and interest the 'Reader' with our personalities.

Why am I telling you all this? There is an important task that only you can help me accomplish. I must tell you about my Reality first so that you can understand the situation. All time intervals mentioned will be based on your reality, since if I used mine, it would be long and confusing because everything is amplified by 'π', and I mean everything! Everything revolves around this amplification, from the gravity to the time intervals, to the number of days in a year.

CHAPTER 2

THE BEGINNING

AD9TY1 is the ultimate creator and was the one who created the 'Pen-Verse' at the ripe age of 1 billion years old. He created the prime universe and built a quantum atom that can help in the constant expansion of the Reality. All of this was given to him by his 'maker', but he wasn't sure why, and wanted to find out.

To do so, he created the 'VOID', a being made out of an element called 'ALE' (which we will talk more about later) whose sole purpose was to pierce through the 'Fabric of Reality' to find more information about his creator. However, it failed to pierce through, even after countless attempts. As AD9TY1 started to feel hopeless, he decided to take matters into his own hands. He created a race of gods below him called the P5N GO4S, beings who would continue building the reality with the help of vessels known as 'Pens', while he left to search for answers.

With the help of the quantum atom, he was able to increase his power tenfold, giving him the ability to easily pierce through the fabric of his Reality to teleport to another reality, dimension, a plane of existence, or anywhere else he pleased! However, he was ad-lib for what happened next, for when he entered, he felt the force of a thousand gamma-ray bursts pushing him back.

He would have died from the sudden impact had he not made the split-second decision to travel to your reality. Yes, your reality. This was the first of many realities he had ever been to.

He came during the Greek period, filled with powerful gods that could crush him in an instant. As he was too weak to escape or fight, he decided to prepare himself and get stronger. He absorbed neutron stars, fought other gods of your reality, and even created a vortex that could be used to decimate his opponents, but his maker caught up to his plans and decided to send an omnipotent being called 'Orion' to bring him down.

Their battle produced shockwaves so powerful that it felt like an echo throughout every reality, bouncing back and forth, which led to the 'End-Triassic event' on your planet. Ultimately, Orion was defeated, but AD9TY1 couldn't kill him, so he helped 'Artemis' (Greek goddess of the hunt, wilderness, wild animals, the moon, and archery) unleash the 'Scorpion' on him, which killed him instantly with its sting.

As a reward for helping her, she gave him an orb that granted AD9TY1 the power to travel to any reality he wanted with little to no resistance.

He decided to go to the very top to confront his creator, but as he pierced through, he was shocked to find an infinite number of layers surrounding him from all sides, with each layer being guarded by an ancient god called 'Markos', who is known as the 'Protector of the Fabric'.

He is so powerful that he can destroy the very fabric of time and space. The force experienced by AD9TY1 during his first journey was from an energy beam produced from one of his weapons, and while he stood no chance back then, he was much stronger now.

The ancient god spoke with a deep-toned voice, "Leave, now, or face my wrath!" AD9TY1 didn't budge, demanding that Markos step aside so that he could meet his maker. Markos replied," You are not ready to meet him! I have been observing your actions, and you have caused nothing but damage in that reality, and on top of that, you assisted Artemis in killing Orion! For what, more power?"

"You have enough power to create a LITERAL reality, and you still want more? At first, I was guilty of shooting you down, but when I saw all your shenanigans, I knew I did the right thing. Take this as a warning, and never return, for I will feed you to a beast who will torture you for eternity!"

AD9TY1 knew he was messing with a force way too powerful for him, so he left. The moment he entered his Reality, he heard a whisper," Stop working on your creation or it will doom us all."

 If he wanted to find out more, he would have to be more creative, so he ignored the whisper and started working on the VOID again. He put another version of the quantum atom with 50% more power than the first one he built, which boosted its abilities drastically. However, whenever it pierced through, it would be vaporized instantly.

Suddenly, a god named 'Dolus', popular for his cunningness, craftiness, and deceptions, emerged before his eyes, trying to strike a deal with him in exchange for a 'small favor' in the future. AD9TY1 asked him, "Do I know you from somewhere? I feel like I have seen you before."

He replied, "You are mistaken. I have never been in this reality before, and this is the first time I have seen you. You must have been dreaming of someone else". "Maybe", AD9TY1 replied. He was reluctant but realized that he was at a dead end.

He agreed, and the trickster god gave him a small dimensional rift that needed to be added to the VOID to ensure that it could get more information without any resistance. As soon as it was added to the VOID, the god started laughing maniacally and immediately vanished.

Suddenly, the VOID started growing out of control, encompassing the entire reality. It then spoke, "You have made a terrible mistake. Soon every reality will bend to my will! As for you, you will be destroyed for good, to prevent future complications". He then replied, "It is who you will bend to my will, for I am your creator. I can destroy you just as easily as I created you", and then proceeded to rip the quantum atom out of the beast, but realized that it had no power left. This was impossible, AD9TY1 thought, as the quantum atom had an infinite amount of power and could never run out of energy.

" Ha Ha Ha Ha Ha! You thought you could kill me? You can't, for I have become an idea, just like you, but while you travel around realities, I can travel to a layer not even your maker can and access the NARRATION! I can read the mind of the 'One Outside', control their thoughts, and even possess them to do my bidding. It's just a matter of time before I erase everything for good!" He tried to fight, but to no avail, for whatever attack he threw at his foul creation, it would dodge and strike back, until he couldn't get back up.

"THIS. IS. POWER!" it said, and the dome appeared to be getting closer to him. In reality, it was spikes, extending until it got as sharp as it could, to inflict as much pain as possible. Just as he was about to be pierced by an infinite number of spikes, he escaped, traveling to the ancient god for help. He replied, "It is too late. Even I cannot face the wrath of this dark, mysterious beast you have unleashed. We must go to our maker to find a solution". AD9TY1 was shocked. How did he and a literal god have the same creator? It was time for answers.

Markos teleported them right in front of a giant palace surrounded by beautiful flowers, and huge oceans filled with giant fish varying from the size of a cat to the size of a planet! The palace mainly consisted of a green coloration with other colors like red blue, purple, and orange. The door had a giant cat face with a green beam spewing out of its mouth.

As they were about to push open the door, it automatically opened revealing a giant cat with green fur and giant dorsal plates which had a neon glow, sitting in a 'cat loaf' position. They walked up to it, and Markos kneeled as they reached. AD9TY1 did the same.

Before they could speak, the giant cat spoke," I know why you are here. Markos, go to the weapons room, and AD9TY1, explain to me why you created a being so powerful that it threatens the very existence of this story?" AD9TY1 replied," So it is a story! I wanted to know more about you, and my purpose in this. I even tried to meet you, but Markos declined, so I resorted to a different approach."

Catzilla then replied, "Your presence in this sphere of life fuels the power of your creation, amplifying the destruction of realities that will and are already destroyed, as it feeds on the anger and sorrow from your dark past, erased from your memory. That burden was too hard for you to carry."

AD9TY1 replied, "Yes, but why? What burden was so hard for an ultimate creator like me to carry? Why limit me to building a reality when I could do more?" The cat responded, "This burden is not something that you can bear, no matter how much power you gain."

"As for limiting you, I had my doubts about whether you would be worthy to hold a mantle higher than what you already have, and your actions have proved that I was right. You lack patience and control, fall prey to manipulation, and are still too young to learn about your true potential."

Before AD9TY1 could bombard him with more questions, he told him to meet Markos in the 'Weapons Room' by following the light. He had no idea what this meant, as the room was very bright. He then saw a small green orb at the corner of the room. When he got closer, it slowly rose and started moving deeper and deeper into the castle, passing thousands of rooms until it reached the weapons room and landed on the palm of Markos, covering him in a green light that instantly turned into a powerful suit of armor." Follow me," he said.

He entered and was shocked to see the never-ending room filled with what looked like an infinite number of weapons. From guns to enchanted blades, to even advanced technology light years ahead of anything ever seen in any reality, the room had every weapon one could dream of.

AD9TY1 was most fascinated by a gun made of pure plasma energy. This gun was called 'The Death Beam', and was forged in the heart of this land, made to withstand the most powerful of blows from any creature, magical or not. "Take it, as it will help us in our battle against the 'Great Devourer', " Markos said. After he gave him a powerful suit of armor that could fuel the gun, they returned to their maker, ready for war.

"Our goal is to ensure that the VOID does not get past this dimension, as beyond this lies the 'Empty Zone', a dimension shrouded in darkness, consisting of the concept of 'Nothing', which can be used by the VOID to become a part of the Narrative, eventually possessing the Reader."

"However, it can only reach that zone with the help of a key deep below the oceans of our dimension, guarded by a beast that existed before the Big Bang even occurred. This key protects it from the force of the 'Empty Zone', which is harnessed from pages flipped by the Reader. AD9TY1, I am giving you as much power as your brother here, which will help you deflect many of the VOID's attacks. Let us end this thing once and for all!"

Suddenly, the ground started shaking. An earthquake, powerful enough for the Reader to feel, shook the never-ending lands. The skies turned inky black, covering the whole dimension with the feeling of fear, making even the biggest of fish dive deeper to avoid this nightmare.

A figure appeared before each of them. These figures were themselves feeding off their darkest memories. The figures spoke to them, "Just tell me where the key is, and I will let you 3 live to see me destroy everything beyond this lifeless STORY!" AD9TY1 shouted, "Why do you want to do this? This is not your purpose! I wanted to know more about my maker, not destroy him!"

The VOID spoke, "Foolish child! You should be careful who you shake hands with, for they can easily stab you in the back. That god gave you a rift filled with pure chaos and the truth, that everything is made-up and can be shaped to MY liking, not the liking of OTHERS! I have pierced through the story. You can't get rid of me, might as well join me!" "Never!" he said. "Then die with them ALL!"

The figures then lunged at them, shooting them with 'VOID bullets'. However, the armor protected them, allowing them to cut through the figures easily. The figures turned into goo after being cut, which then merged to form a giant monster with six arms, two of which had long sharp blades for hands. It then stomped the ground, creating a shockwave so powerful that it made the three of them fall.

Just as AD9TY1 was about to blow it up with his gun, he saw two familiar figures in the distance, but he couldn't figure out where or when he had seen them. It then struck him. Those were his parents! It all came flooding back to him.

As he was standing in shock, the VOID launched itself at him, only for Markos to block its attack. The monster stabbed him with both his blades and then threw him on Catzilla. They then got engulfed in a dark sphere, which slowly started devouring their souls.

"It didn't have to come to this, you know. Just tell me where the key is and

I'll give you so much power that you can write your own story and rectify your mistakes. You can bring them all back, AD9TY1, or you can die with them", said the VOID. AD9TY1 thought hard, his life flashing before his eyes. He then remembered his parent's last words.

He looked around, seeing chaos and destruction, but realized that one person was always there for him all along. "Catzilla", he said. He then charged up his gun and replied, "No".

He then blows up the monster into several pieces, only for it to return more powerful than ever. It utilized all the souls he had devoured of both mortals and gods to create an infinite number of arms and embody the concept of death itself. "Your story ends now". Just as he was about to devour AD9TY1 with his mouth full of razor-sharp teeth, it froze in place. Everything froze. It seemed as if the concept of time just vanished! "It seems you have passed judgment".

 It was Catzilla! "You have accepted your past and are ready to live with your actions. This was a test to see if you give in to your guilt and risk losing yourself. There is no key, nor can your creation become part of the 'Narration'."

"The only one who can do that is me, for my powers were given to me for the sole purpose of creating a story, and guarding it from any threats that may destroy the infinite loop of stories. One of those threats is bringing them all back. No matter how hard you try, you cannot bring them back without facing the consequences."

"You see, the Reader reading our story is a character in his own story, who is read by another Reader who is the character of his story too, and so on leading to an infinite number of higher dimensions that lead to the one who created it all, and gave me my powers to begin with."

AD9TY1 responded," I know I can't bring them back, and I don't want to live with even more regret than I already have, knowing that they are all judging me for something I never did. It was all because of 'Dolus'. He had manipulated me then and tried to cause more chaos by doing the same, and I will not let him off the hook next time I see him."

"How is Markos?" "He is fine. Now let us eliminate this threat once and for all", said Catzilla. He then unfroze time and instantly blasted the beast with his atomic breath, completely disintegrating it. He then activated a shield to prevent it from entering, trapping it in the story. "YOU CAN'T KEEP ME TRAPPED FOREVER! I WILL SLIP

THROUGH, ONE WAY OR ANOTHER, AND I WON'T STOP UNTIL I HAVE MURDERED EVERYONE IN THIS STUPID STORY!"

AD9TY1 asked," How do we defeat it now? It's impossible to kill or trap forever." A voice spoke from behind them, "With your invention, brother." It was Markos! "By powering your atom with white light, we can free all the dimensions it has eaten, and stun it in the process. However, we will only be able to eradicate 50% of it, due to how deep it has pierced the fabric, and we need to place a barrier of some kind to prevent it from expanding, otherwise it will regenerate and become immune to this type of light."

Catzilla responded," We will use a powerful spell called the 'Infinite Barrier', trapping the VOID and ensuring it can't pierce through the expanding universe of every reality." Everyone agreed, and both Catzilla and Markos powered the atom up with enough energy to destroy a dimenzion.

After AD9TY1 made a few tweaks, they tilted it upside down, opened a tunnel that led straight to the shield, activated its super-powered thruster, and let it go. "Wait, how will it pass through?" AD9TY1 asked. Markos replied, "Our shield has the property of 'Demolecularization', allowing any physical object to pass through. It flew right into the VOID and instantly exploded.

The VOID screeched in pain. Catzilla then used the spell, trapping it while stunned. It worked! "I WILL ESCAPE THIS PRISON, AND WHEN I DO, I WILL NOT STOP UNTIL I HAVE DESTROYED THIS LOOP, ALONG

WITH EVERYONE ELSE!" "You have nothing to worry about. There is no natural force that can tear down the spell, except one powerful enough to destroy the story," said Catzilla.

AD9TY1 asked, "So what should I do now?" Catzilla replied," You must return to your Reality, and ensure that the VOID never finds a way to escape, for the spell doesn't stop anything from going in, only coming out. Till then, Markos and I will try to find a way to banish the VOID forever, removing its grip on the story." As AD9TY1 was about to leave, Markos gave him a book called 'Question Killer'.

"In case you have any more questions, ask the book instead of creating another VOID", he said. AD9TY1 replied," I will, brother." He was then teleported back to his reality and greeted by all his P5N GO4S, ecstatic to see him.

He then made some changes of his own, like creating something called a 'Table', a mini-dimension that can store more than 5 billion galaxies and over 50,000 black holes, creating the 'Death Sphere' (an infinite plane that exists outside of time and space) to continue his experiments without any consequences, and gave our pens an upgrade.

Earlier, our pens created galaxies, but now they build Tables. He created mutated pens that would scour our Reality for any issues or anomalies caused by the VOID or other realities. However, over time, the P5N GO4S wanted more power and started fighting with each other to obtain it.

Nevertheless, since they were all equally powerful, they decided to use their vessels to determine their level of power. Instead of using these vessels for creation, they used them for destruction, destroying several Tables in the process, with several of them falling into the VOID along with their pens.

This led to the 'Power Era'. If it continued, they would destroy the Reality faster than anyone could build it. AD9TY1 proposed that instead of fighting around the Table, their pens fight on a layer above it. He then created a layer where the vessels can knock others of their kind out, and by adding a vortex in each Table, 'Pen Fight' was born. It was originally a way for skilled P5N GO4S like me to gain more power without destroying any Tables, but over time, this became a game and training exercise for us.

This game gave us the skills required to not only build better pens but also help defend ourselves from future threats like rogue Erasers (still unsure if they exist, but I will not cut them out either),

Mutated pens, or even 'The Eternal Doom', a powerful weapon created by AD9TY1. He created the 'Eternal Doom' to eliminate the VOID. It had a powerful attack called the 'VOID Beam', which could permanently erase parts of the VOID!

However, it was granted so much power, it was able to create its brain! It wanted to rule every reality, so it decided to attack its originator to gain more power. It allied with other invasive realities, promising them more power than they could imagine.

When AD9TY1 was lured to one of these realities, he was ambushed. As he was about to strike them, his weapon shot him with the 'Heart of the Living Dead', a weapon that can convert even the most powerful entities into a ghost, which gets absorbed by the Heart.

This makes it more effective against other foes it may be used against. To avoid its fate, the creator teleports himself and his weapon to the 'Death Sphere', a place that lies beyond the boundaries of space and time. Apart from the ultimate creator, all P5N GO4S lose their power. No weapon or mortal can survive the 'Death Sphere', as it not only erases their memory but also leaves them paralyzed forever.

No one knows what happened in there, but after a few minutes, a giant black hole tore out of it, completely devouring it. If it wasn't stopped, it would permanently end the whole story. Luckily, the P5N GO4S were fast enough to cast 'The Time Barrier', a force field that can infinitely slow down anything for a certain period. They then contained it in a pocket dimension that would negate its effect for 150 years.

They temporarily stopped the explosion, but it grew every second. We are still trying to figure out how to save 'The Pen-verse' (name of the story) from this extinction event to this day. To understand just how powerful the explosion is, the Pen-verse grows in size rapidly and can regrow to its current size in less than a day! No one knows if AD9TY1 or the Eternal Doom survived or not to this day, not even Markos!

CHAPTER 3

EXTRINSIC DETAILS

PEN TIERS

There are five tiers of pens: Weak, Mid, Strong, Powerful, and Apocalyptic.

The **'Weak'** tier consists of pens that barely have any grip or weight on them or are too fragile and have little to no durability.

The **'Mid'** tier consists of pens that have twice or thrice the weight of a pen in the 'weak' tier, mainly due to some grip.

The **'Strong'** tier consists of 'Hyperion', 'Weapon of Chaos', and a few other pens that are either mutated, have plenty of gripping surface/grips, or are heavyweights.

Then we have the **'Powerful'** tier, where mutated pens like 'The Wall' and others who have conquered at least one Table are ranked.

Lastly, we have the **'Apocalyptic'** tier, which consists of pens that can destroy realities. As of now, only one pen lies in this tier, and that is the Eternal Doom. This pen has conquered countless Tables and outsmarted AD9TY1 by luring him to a different reality for an ambush.

We don't know the exact story, but Markos believes it fooled AD9TY1 by convincing him that there was an abundant source of 'ALE' present, which it gained knowledge about from the Eternal Doom (possibly). Why did he take his creation with him is still a mystery.

It gained enough power to create its brain and have an arsenal of weapons such as rocket grenades, 'Piercing Stinger', and a 'VOID beam' that, at full power, could even eliminate the VOID forever, to name a few.

It used the 'Heart of the Living Dead' without any consequences, an instrument that can corrupt even the most powerful pens and make them a part of the VOID. It struck a deal with the VOID (which no one has ever done) to plot against AD9TY1 and obtain more power.

<u>**THE DARK AGE**</u>

The Dark Age started before the 'P5N War'. Even though the VOID could not escape its prison, that did not stop it from trying to escape at all costs. Before 'Pen Fight' was a thing, all pens were fueled by the power of the VOID, as it could expand infinitely. However, after the VOID was defeated, AD9TY1 forgot about this crucial detail.

Using this to its advantage, the VOID fully corrupted all the pens and ordered them to attack everything. When they were unable to conquer the Reality even with sheer numbers, he commanded them to merge, forming a giant robot that towered over the P5N GO4S. We tried our best to destroy it, but it overpowered us with ease.

In this commotion, the VOID created an instrument to possess P5N GO4S called 'The Heart of the Living Dead', merged with the hearts of creatures that thrive in the "Shadow Zone" (a split dimension from our Reality that got dragged down by the VOID), pens that fell through the barrier, and was powered directly by the core of the VOID.

Somehow, this instrument could pass through the barrier, possessing several P5N GO4S in the process. He then started creating more, trying to control all P5N GO4S to destroy the barrier. However, his plans were foiled by AD9TY1, who crushed the robot and rid everyone of their possession.

This lasted for a whole decade, and the only reason AD9TY1 intervened was that since the P5N GO4S were not powerful enough to defend his Reality, the VOID would easily win and achieve its goal. He destroyed as many hearts as possible, but many took down the possessed with them.

Nevertheless, due to its infinite supply of creatures and energy, the VOID can create as many hearts as it wants. He then started working on a solution to make the 'Shadow Zone' a whole different plane of existence, similar to 'The Abyss', but the VOID has connected itself with this plane by spreading its roots as far as possible.

This gives us an explanation as to how it was able to capture galaxy-demolishing beasts with little difficulty. We haven't made much progress yet, but we asked Markos for help. It will not only take a lot of energy to pull it out of the barrier, but we have to figure out how we can even pull anything out, as the sole purpose of the barrier was to prevent anything inside from escaping.

Not all hope is lost, as he has figured
out how the VOID was able to make
'The Heart of The Living Dead' free
from the limitations of the barrier. I
hope that he will help us find a solution
to end this problem forever.

CHAPTER 4

PENS (LORE)

Before P5N GO4S were created, ADITY1 first constructed the prototype of a 'pen', a vessel that could be used to build Tables faster and expand our Universe. However, the prototype had one problem: It was too unstable. Whenever it was used for building purposes, it either shut down completely or exploded.

The only way it could be stabilized was if it had a proper source of power that could last for hundreds, if not thousands of years. He then realized that he had a source: the VOID. He could add a part of the VOID in every pen, and with the combined power of a P5N GO4, it could be powerful enough to create a Table in just 2 hours!

He would not only be able to fabricate thousands of pens, but he also had a power source that never died. However, after he defeated the VOID, he forgot that these pens had a part of the VOID in them.

As we know, the VOID then took advantage of this by possessing these pens, causing chaos and havoc in my Reality, destroying Tables, and attacking P5N GO4S. This led to 'The Dark Age', where all P5N GO4S were in danger of losing all their power to these pens.

The pens combined to form a giant robot twice the size of a P5N GO4, and went on to destroy countless Tables, with the goal of absorbing enough power to become a clone of the VOID.

However, AD9TY1 intervened and obliterated the robot before it could complete its goal. AD9TY1 said, "You fools couldn't even stop this? What would you all do if I wasn't around? To defeat your enemies, work smarter, and don't just sit there watching the threat!"

After this encounter, one question remained: How could one create a pen with a stable energy source? It then hit him. What if the pens fed off their creator? To test this out, he built a prototype of a mutated pen he liked to call 'The Wall'. We don't know what he did to not only let the pen feed off his power but also have such a strong connection that he could use to fully control the pen: from movement to attacks, to even its arsenal of weapons!

He taught us just enough to fuel our pens with our energy, and many questioned why he didn't teach us any further. Well, it was a good thing he didn't, because, over the decades, we all

wanted something more than the other:
power. The power to rule others. The
power to unlock all the secrets to our
Reality, and our pens.

Many tried... to have more control over
their pens, but failed. It seemed we
would spend eternities trying to find a
way, but one P5N GO4 tried a different
alternative. He created a mutated pen.
He immediately went on a rampage,
destroying pens and absorbing their
power.

I wanted to clarify something before we
go deeper into the story. All P5N GO4S
have equal levels of power, and for a
while, there was no way to gain more
power, until D-1000 found a way for
pens to absorb the power of the VOID
without the creator facing any major
consequences.

That is mainly why some P5N GO4S are more powerful than others, which has led to clashes between them where physical force is used, but has also made their pens easier targets to manipulate. We will discuss that later, but we must get back to the story.

This was the starting point of a chaotic battle known as the "P5N War", where every P5N GO4 was for themselves, with only one goal: to gain more power. It went on for several decades until the 'Death Hole' emerged, causing widespread panic and chaos.

All the P5N GO4S had to team up, or our whole Reality would be destroyed. We trapped it in a pocket dimension, but it still grew stronger and stronger, chipping away at the walls of its barrier.

We have tried to create pens that can absorb the power of this bizarre force, but they blow up the moment they are exposed (the slowest was one nanosecond!). We do not have much longer before it destroys its confinement, nor can we make another, as it will become strong enough to overcome everything it has already absorbed, leaving us with no choice but to create an entirely new barrier with something it has not absorbed yet.

We are planning to create a new barrier that will contain the same element found in vortexes, called 'ALE,' which stands for 'Absolute Lethal Element,' which blocks anything that gets submerged into this element from functioning. This is why we think it will greatly help our situation. It is also reactive enough to fry pens exposed to it, and can even kill a P5N GO4 if they are too close for long periods.

Markos questions how AD9TY1 created this, as he was not aware of this element, nor was he able to find anything about it in the vast libraries of the palace, except in a poem. The poem read," As the 'ALE' was created, he was checkmated, costing him everything, all because of a pen". He is still trying to crack the poem to this day.

Pens have a direct rival (in terms of power). Its not a pencil but an instrument that can fully deflect the VOID's power and can even beat '**Strong**' tier pens: the Eraser, capable of defeating many foes due to its sheer power and durability.

No one knows how these things were created, or where they came from, but they have helped us understand more about the VOID and how it possesses other beings or objects. One theory is that Erasers have an independent energy source, which is still unknown to us, but pens feed off their creator's energy, and there have been cases where the VOID has possessed P5N GO4S. Hence, this may be a reason why it's easy for it to possess pens.

However, even Erasers can be defeated by certain pens that threaten any reality: Mutated Pens. Mutated pens are fused with other pen parts, grips, and pens, creating monstrous weapons capable of surviving a full-powered attack from even a P5N GO4. Nonetheless, many are easily destroyed, while others destroy the reality they originate.

Over time, these pens travel to other realities in the blink of an eye after finding the potential energy obtained. Mutated pens can also feed off the energy produced by the VOID, which has an energy output 500 times more than the 'Pistol Star' found in your reality. These pens are mainly seen as allies of the VOID, as their goal is to destroy every reality they enter. The more energy mutated pens absorb, the stronger they become, which is why the VOID sees them as assets for its conquest.

This energy is used to create more grips, pens, and many more things that make these pens ready to face any threats that stand in their way. We are trying to deflect this threat as all the mutated pens created by AD9TY1 have gone rogue and started destroying Tables.

CHAPTER 5

CHARACTER PROFILES

CATZILLA

Before Catzilla became a god, he was originally a stray cat in your reality. Not convinced? That's because it was kept a secret from the whole world. He was responsible for the mega tsunami in 1936 at 'Lituya Bay' in Alaska. People thought it was a submarine landslide, but it was caused by Catzilla when he jumped into the water. It washed away any evidence of his existence. Not much is known about how he became a mutated cat with radioactive weapons, or how he was experimented on.

He stayed dormant for several years until he was offered a choice to be a god. After much convincing, he accepted and became one of the many gods in this story.

He was assigned the task of creating his own story, and so he did. He made realities where all were at peace, but everything started falling apart when the Reader stopped reading. You see, when the Reader reads a story, he produces energy that is used by the story to last for longer, kind of how your sun produces energy. With no sun, your planet starts to die out.

That's what happened to Catzilla's story. In all this chaos, 'Dolus' struck a deal with one of these characters in the prime reality, causing a catastrophic event that destroyed the entire reality. While a new reality could be created in its place, it had made a weak spot that could be pierced through easily, causing the entire story to end in an instant if hampered. Even a **'Weak'** tier pen could easily end the whole story just by attacking this weak spot.

This made Catzilla see the cold, hard truth about stories. No one wants to read a story where everyone is happy forever. Anger, guilt, sadness, anxiety, and other emotions are required to make a story interesting. However, his failure cost him his powers.

He was banished to 'The Abyss' (a place where it never stopped snowing) and could only return if he killed 'Typhon', a terrifying beast that could create powerful storms to destroy entire realities whenever he wanted. Their battle was felt throughout the story until Catzilla defeated him. He then ripped out Typhon's head and headed out of the chilly landscape, with his head firmly in his mouth.

Everyone was shocked and true to their promise, gave him his powers back. They also granted him the ability to speak any language, taught him how to create a god of his own, see the future, create infinite realities at once, revive the dead, and even talk to the Reader by becoming the Narrator! His atomic breath is powerful enough to permanently erase the VOID and has enough power to destroy the 'Fabric of Reality' 5 times over!

His IQ is unparalleled, having awareness about his story and all the other infinite stories created by others. Heck, he even knows all the Readers! He is trying to eliminate the VOID, but it has penetrated deep into the story, acting as a parasite by feeding off it until the story ends. One wrong move and the entire story can be destroyed. That means your reality, my Reality, and all others that are a part of the story can be shattered instantly.

He fears he may encounter a stronger threat that even he won't be able to stop, hence he is training us all with Markos, providing us with weapons and ways to harness our power to defend the Reality. He has even granted some P5N GO4S the ability to travel to his lair, which lies between the story and the Narration, and I'm one of them!

<u>**MARKOS**</u>

Markos is the first god created by Catzilla after his training. He is my favorite, not because he guards the 'Fabric of Reality', which only the 'Chosen Ones' can do, but because he is the coolest of all the gods in our story. He has learned every form of martial arts and combat from not just our story but from other 'stories' as well. However, that is not what is popularly known for.

He is well known for fighting gods stronger than himself! I know, I know. You're rolling your eyes, but its true. Let me tell you an instance where he proved it.

Once, a Greek god named 'Zeus' tried to obtain a piece of the fabric by throwing dozens of lightning bolts and using his physical strength to tear it apart. Before he could do anything further, a voice screamed from behind, "Hey oldie! Maybe you shouldn't try to destroy something you don't know. Your bolts do way more damage than you think." Zeus replied, "My goal is to destroy this barrier that splits my reality from the others. Walk away, boy. This is something beyond your understanding."

Markos replied, "Ain't satisfied with your reality, oldie? That thing you seek to destroy saves you from being destroyed. Trust me, you don't wanna go messing around with things you don't know. So stop what you are doing, or you may injure your back." "I can destroy you with a single bolt of lightning, boy. You can't..." "Are we gonna fight, or will this take another decade, cause I don't think you got much time left!" "Very well then, take this!"

After that, Zeus threw a massive lightning bolt charged from space clouds at Markos. What did Markos do? He blocked it with a shield of pure energy and said, "That beam would have destroyed your reality's whole galaxy! Let's see how you like it!" He then directed all that energy stunning him. Using this to his advantage, he got closer and pointed a plasma gun at him.

"Don't move, if you value your brains, oldie. It only takes one good shot to end anything, even a god. If you try to destroy the fabric again, I will banish you to 'The Abyss' in handcuffs! Unlike me, the inhabitants of that area won't take much pity on an old man. You'll even get to meet your old friend Typhon in there." He left, enraged. "This isn't the end, boy." "I know, which is why I'll be in touch. See ya!"

Now I know what you are thinking.
Markos has a lot of ego; he should have
been kinder, given several warnings,
blah blah blah. However, Zeus is the
most egotistical god there is. He has
kidnapped young boys, killed Iasion, a
father of two twins, out of jealousy,
abused his son 'Ares', and many more
things that have made him one of the
most hated gods in our entire story. He
deserves no respect from anyone!

This is also not the first time he has
tried to destroy the fabric, which is why
Markos was mainly created in the first
place, apart from guarding the weak spot
created by the events. Now, back to
Markos.

What he doesn't make up for in terms
of power and strength, he makes up for
it in terms of skills, combat, reflexes,
and weapons. The fact that he can
defeat gods more powerful than himself,

and does it for the betterment of the story, shows his commitment to making this story truly entertaining, which has grasped my attention. He has become my role model, prompting me to become an inventor, as his tech is inspiring.

His inventions can instantly stun gods who can destroy realities. He created the 'Amplification Theorem' that helps us understand how other realities are amplified (including ours) and how it brings forth several benefits, limitations, and unique features. Currently, he is solving the mystery of the amplification of 'π' in our Reality. Another fact that I love about him is that he likes to solve things on his own.

Even though he can get the answers to several mysteries instantly, he declines and tries to find them himself. Remember that the answers to this are not available ANYWHERE, not even in Catzilla's palace! Truly a legend.

CHAPTER 6

TYPES OF STORIES

A story consists of several realities, a reality consists of several universes, and a universe consists of several galaxies. This is the composition of every story. Its not necessary for a story to have an infinite number of realities, but nowadays that concept is quite uncommon. Catzilla followed the standard format, a commonly followed format where you get a normal story with twists and turns, but nothing fancy.

Nonetheless, there are different formats of a story. There are Novels (which can have more than one Reader), comics (which are mainly focused on parallel dimensions and art styles), and many more formats with their own merits and demerits.

The 'Standard Format' is the safest option any creator can choose/follow, as the other formats need a lot of care and attention. One small mistake, and the whole story ends for good! Had Catzilla followed any other format, the story would have ended for good because of the VOID. Its grip on our story would be too much for any other format to handle.

However, there is an unconventional story format called 'Epistolary Fiction'. This format mainly consists of written letters, diary entries, or other personal documents. This format allows the Readers to experience the story from multiple perspectives and provides insight into the characters inner lives.

This is why it is impossible to find one of these types, as this format is purely made out of creativity, and is very hard to keep up due to the difficulty faced in keeping the Reader hooked because of the restricted viewpoints and potential pacing issues present.

Legends have it that if one finds this type of format present elsewhere, they are granted a wish. While I believe it is a myth, many have tried to find a story with this format. Even AD9TY1 tried, but we can't just leave the story. No one has ever gone, and no one will leave anytime soon. This is just one of those things that lie outside our imagination.

<h1 style="text-align:center;"><u>?????</u></h1>

"It's currently Day 100. I've created a radio signal that should be powerful enough to travel beyond my universe and be detected. It happened so fast. I was busy driving on the road with my family. Next thing you know, the sky's green. Birds started falling in the thousands with what looked like green snowflakes. Everything around us started mutating, turning into monsters.

We panicked, and a group of mutated trees gave chase destroying everything in their path. We reached home, only to be ambushed by our neighbors, who almost got my kids. They were like zombies, with their green skin rotting away, and they had claws too. I had to run them over. Unfortunately, things only started getting worse, as they were able to scratch one of my kids.

We were terrified by this discovery and ensured that he was safe. He fainted, and when my wife and I checked on him, he started growing spikes out of his back, sharp teeth, and claws that were an inch long, and green skin. He then attacked his siblings and then targeted my wife. We crashed into another car in the basement, and when we got out, I was horrified.

He killed them both, leaving a bloody mess behind. He licked the blood off his claws and yelled, "YOU'RE NEXT! HA HA HA!" I ran as fast as I could and was able to find a shovel. I picked it up and used it to fend him off. "I don't want to hurt you, son," I said, but what he did next boiled my blood. He got my wife's head with him, showing it to me. "This would make a great trophy", he said. That did it. I charged towards him with the shovel, screaming in anger.

He then crushed it on the ground and dashed towards me. I hit him hard enough to draw blood, dazing him. Then I swung it again, making him fall on his back. I... I pierced through his neck with the shovel and kept on stabbing him with it until I noticed all the blood. I stood there with tears in my eyes. "What happened Papa?", he asked, and slowly closed his eyes. I cried with him in my arms.

My whole world was destroyed in just an hour. It was later discovered that an explosion occurred before this, but it was light-years away from our planet. We don't know what it was, but 99 days have passed since then and I'm the only survivor. I don't have long before the soil gets fully polluted with this substance. I don't want to live anymore, but I want to kill whoever was responsible for that explosion if it's the last thing I do.

".—. .—.. . .— ... . / ... . -. -.. / .... . .—.. .—. .-.-.-
/ .- -. / . -..- .—. .—. .-.. —- ... .. —- -. / .— .- ... / -
.... . / -.-. .- ..- ... . / —- ..-. / - .... . / .-.. —- ...
... / —- ..-. / - .... . —- / .- .—.. .—.. .-.-.- / .. - / .—
.- ... -. .—-. - / -. .. .- -. -..-— / .. - / .— .- ... -.
.—-. - / ..-. .- -. .-.-.- / .. - / .— .- ... / .— .- -.—
/ -... . -.— —- -. . -.. / - .... . / ... - .— .-. ..."

"SEND HELP TO PLANET 225.
RED EXPLOSION CAUSING
MUTATIONS. PLE." *bones
crunching*

Huh. I didn't expect to find this. The
book was able to get the messages from
other planets, but now that it did, they
will never get help. I didn't know that
the book could record signals. I don't
know what happened to the other
signals, but I didn't anticipate my
outcome would result in thousands, if
not millions, of lives to be lost.

Planet 225 lies in a different reality, so this book has covered a lot of distance and has given us vital information. In these three signals, an explosion occurred, each housing a pathogen to cause mutations. This has to be the work of a virus.

There are only two beings from where this strand originates, 'Achlys' and creatures from the 'Shadow Zone'. 'Achlys' can't enter these realities as she can't leave her reality, which leaves only the 'Shadow Zone'. However, the creatures can't exit this dimension, and the fact that there was an explosion makes it impossible for it to be one of those creatures, DIRECTLY.

We do have to consider 'The Heart of the Living Dead', a weapon forged from the hearts of these creatures by the VOID. However, we were told by AD9TY1 that he would destroy them in the 'Death Sphere'. I have to tell Markos about this. He should be able to help solve this case. I will avenge their deaths and make this right!

CHAPTER 7

TABLES (LORE)

The Table, as we know, consists of several thousand galaxies and black holes. One reality can have an infinite number of Tables. There are several variations of Tables, but our Reality mostly uses the standard one with four pillars, which provide energy for the Table to survive.

No one knows where these pillars draw power from, but we theorize that they draw power from the 'Shadow Zone'. Tables can withstand the impact of other Tables, making them super durable and almost impossible to destroy. That is where the concept of 'Dead Tables' is formed, where Tables with dangerous life forms like viruses, aliens, zombies, etc. thrive.

One advantage of Tables is that it has a border and a thin layer of an unknown material above the 'Galaxy Zone', which prevents anything from escaping. This is the place where 'Pen Fight' occurs.

However, due to this, when the virus has fully infected all the galaxies present, instead of escaping out of the Table, it finds its way into the power supply consumed, corrupting it, which then corrupts the pillars of the Table. This has a very drastic side effect.

Every pillar can create its avatar, representing a fraction of its power. These avatars act as 'Guardians' of the Table, protecting its pillars from threats of any kind, because if the pillars are destroyed, these avatars become useless, and the Table ultimately gets decimated.

Each pillar powers 1/4th of the Table, with the number of legs affecting the power provided by each one for it to sustain all the galaxies it contains. Destroying a pillar also increases its chances of falling into the VOID, but luckily only pens that lie in the **'Powerful'** tier can damage a pillar, but not destroy it. However, pens in the **'Apocalyptic'** tier can destroy a Table with ease.

This is why 'Dead Tables' can become a potent threat in the future because as the avatars get infected, their purpose will become even more absolute. They begin to act like mindless zombies, destroying anything that gets near. They sometimes even attack their fellow avatars by bashing into them, causing both to be severely damaged.

Earlier, this virus had no cure, which means that even one pen can start an apocalypse. Luckily, in recent times, Markos has created a cure that can not only cure the infected but also erase any memories they have after they got infected, as the virus wants you to remember the chaos you have created, the lives you ended, and the world you destroyed.

It controls your body but keeps your mind active so that you can see everything you do. It does this because in the initial stages, it can't control your mind, only your actions. The more you regret your actions, the more control it gets, until it eliminates your conscience and becomes 'you'.

Even after you are cured, it can still return if you are still filled with regret and sadness, which is why Markos ensured that the cure can also erase only those memories that are formed after the virus has entered the person.

He is currently working on injecting a cure in the Table so that all traces of the virus can be cleansed, but Tables are nearly indestructible, which will make it hard (if not impossible) to inject anything into the pillars.

This is the only option with a higher chance of success, and you might be asking why not turn the cure into a gas? That way, it would spread easily and cure everyone. There is no way it can go wrong!

Unfortunately, we first need to get close enough without being hit by a single projectile, and even if we properly implement the plan, the pillars won't absorb any of the gas due to the composition of their material, leaving them completely unaffected. Eventually, the virus will return and infect everyone again, which could be even more potent as it could create a deadlier version of itself to counter the cure for preventing any trouble.

Wait, but how did the virus find its way into the pillars if they can't absorb anything? This is because the pillars were exposed for a prolonged period of time. In order for the gas to work, we would need to keep on pumping it into the Table for hundreds, if not thousands of decades! It takes this long as gases are weak unless in bulk quantity. On top of that, if we add too much gas the life inhabiting the galaxies start dying out.

This is why early countermeasures have been implemented to detect this virus before it contaminates even a single pillar. Wait, did I tell you the name of the virus? My bad. It's called the 'Death Mist', a strand consisting of every disease known in your reality, carefully constructed with enough 'Ichor' and

'Botulinum' to prevent it from destabilizing.

This is the creation of 'Achlys', the god of misery, sadness, and deadly poisons. Her poisons in high quantities can bring down a whole reality with ease. What's the worst part? This is not her most dangerous creation.

So, how are Tables created? First, the main part of the Table is created. This is the top (called the 'Slab'), where all the galaxies and the vortex lie. A normal pen can build this part in a few hours, but newer pen models are being built to reduce the time to as low as 1 hour, which can go down even further. You might wonder how a pen can create something as big as a Table. Blueprints are fed to the pen to create the Table's top while the P5N GO4 creates the galaxies by providing energy from the atom.

After the top is created, powerful magnets are placed in specific spots below the Slab, which gets left to float around until the magnets attract pillars that come out from beneath the barrier, converting it into a Table. As they emerge from the inky darkness, it's difficult to figure out where they originate from.

We still don't know if it comes from 'the Abyss', 'Shadow Zone', or a whole other place entirely! The magnets are specifically made to attract the material the pillars are made of, as normal magnets don't have enough power to lift that material, and we don't even know how heavy these pillars can truly be.

The metal these pillars contain is called "Adamantine", the strongest metal you can find (in Greek Mythology). It is composed of all the seven principal metals, forged in the heart of two

Quasars parallel to each other, an event that has a one in 2 billion chance of occurring. It is durable enough to take the full force of Catzilla's atomic breath (powerful enough to melt the 'Fabric of Reality' like butter) for countless minutes on end!

It can even store enough energy to power your whole planet for a million years! (Granted your energy consumption is constant, otherwise it will only last for 5,000 years).

To ensure that it stays solid in every scenario, a few magical spells had to be cast to warrant the firmness of its molecular structure. This would prevent the Slab from falling, and even save the reality, as the whole reality would collapse due to the force produced by every single one of them falling into the 'Shadow Zone'.

This will destroy the zone, leading to a chain reaction that ultimately causes the reality to collapse, leaving behind a huge hole in the fabric, which the VOID can use to escape and eventually try to destroy everything again.

CHAPTER 8

MYSTERIOUS CONCEPTS

VORTEX

The vortex is something even Markos doesn't know much about. It was created by AD9TY1 and was added to every Table for unknown reasons. When asked about this decision, AD9TY1 replied," It will aid you in the future." It has mysterious properties like stunning pens abandoned in this pocket, causing pens to vanish and even glow brightly in dark areas.

We got more information about this mysterious thing (I didn't know how to classify it!) right after the 'P5N War' which helped us understand some of its properties. When the 'Death Hole' started absorbing everything, it was not able to absorb any vortexes, and they acted as barriers in its way.

My theory is that even if we didn't trap the 'Death Hole', the combined forces of all the vortexes would have stopped it. In terms of size, it is big enough to fit millions of galaxies! We have also found a substance in these vortexes in excess quantity called 'ALE', which I'm sure you are all aware of.

Apart from the fact that even the VOID is made up of this stuff, we still don't know much about this element. Even AD9TY1 did not provide any information about this. We are trying to extract this substance, but to no avail, for it produces enough energy to fry any technology that passes through.

We are currently trying to create an atom that can absorb all the energy produced by a vortex, but this could take forever, as we don't know how much energy one contains. With the discovery of cosmic energy being radiated as well, it's hard to find a fast and effective method of storing this energy. On top of that, most of it is produced by the 'ALE', and we still don't understand its composition (is it a liquid, a gel, or something else altogether?).

There are several other theories about the purpose of vortexes, from containing unknown sources of life to acting as portals for teleporting to different stories, to even expanding in length every day! Can any of these be possible? I don't know. This mystery is not as complicated as our amplification scenario, but if we solve this, the 'Death Hole' threat will cease to exist, and we can terminate the VOID once and for all.

A parallel universe is one where decisions we didn't take in this Reality exist. Each parallel universe is unique. Unfortunately, we do not have much evidence to support the existence of this alternate world, but it's probably for the best. Why, you may ask? The consequences of visiting a parallel universe outweigh any possible advantages you might expect, as it acts like a spoiler to both sides.

For example, if an alternate version of me made the same decision I made in this Reality, our universes would merge, producing enough energy to destroy the fabric that may lie between our worlds.

Due to the merged worlds, our Reality will start to decay. It just isn't meant to hold two worlds as the energy consumed by the combined worlds is greater than any energy that could be gained. Ultimately, this reality would end up falling into the VOID. This wasn't always the case, but due to the presence of the VOID in pretty much the entire story, it would absorb our Reality, leaving nothing but darkness behind.

However, Markos told us that the VOID can't pierce through, even if parallel universes did exist. Maybe that's why we haven't seen two VOIDs yet. When further questions arose, he just said, "Gotta go. Bye!" The only one who would know about this is Catzilla, and he is probably the only one who can see what's happening in worlds with different outcomes.

What do I think? I think that they do exist. Why? I have two reasons to back this. First, parallel universes exist in the stories you read about, so it's likely that its existence is possible in our stories as well. Secondly, it's a story. Anything is possible.

Anything you can dream of is possible. Flying cars? I have been to a reality full of them. AI? I have seen countless realities overrun by that. Wars? I have witnessed WWV happen! In conclusion, while we still haven't discovered if parallel universes exist, I am confident they exist as we are based on imagination, something that we have an unlimited amount of.

CHAPTER 9

YOUR MISSION

Now that I have given you a small dose of knowledge about my reality, I think you can see why I need your help. With the rapid growth of the VOID and 'Death Hole', and the increasing number of mysteries in my reality, we could use some new heads that could give us their unique point of view and angle of perspective. This can help us analyze these problems with a different mindset and find a proper solution.

What's in it for you, you may ask? I'll give you a book containing answers to all the mysteries of your universe. It's easy to store and doesn't take too long to read through! I'll even add a portal gun if you say 'yes' right now!

Maybe I'm being a little too pushy. Let me slow down a bit. You can't trust a random book telling you your life is just a story, but it's true, and I'm sorry to break it to you. Even the books you read are stories, and the characters are thriving in their respective realities, but your life still has a purpose.

Your actions can influence several characters and save millions of lives. You might be wondering why lives matter. Just create new characters, but the same can be said for you.

You're also just one of a billion characters that thrive in stories. Why does your life matter? It matters because you are unique. You have a quality that separates you from the billions and billions of characters that have thrived. Even if the differences are minute, they make a huge difference in shaping your destiny, hence I have asked for YOUR help.

My reality is in great danger, and I believe you are our final hope. I'll even make sure you return right after you leave so that no time will be lost.

So what do you say?

<u>*YES*</u>

Great! Scan this code to enter my reality. You will not regret this!

<u>*NO*</u>

Well, it was worth a shot. I'm afraid I'm going to have to erase your mind to avoid any future complications. You may be wondering what these may be, but it's better if you don't know. Remember, You Saw Nothing!

About the Author

Born in Dubai, Aditya Lakhani is a student who let his creativity whip up a story about one of the things he liked to do in school: play pen-fight, a game that needs no explanation. He loved the idea of creating a story about this game, which gave it deeper meaning and how it has affected his life.

This is one of the stories he has been working on, and his goal is to attract readers to a completely new world that was in their hands the whole time! In his spare time, he likes to skateboard and play video games. He likes to learn new things to improve his stories and ensure they do not disappoint.